W9-BMR-287

Now I live all alone at the Top of the World. It's a very tall mountain. I can see to the edge. The days are slow and fine. I eat hardtack and gristle. I dust the rocks and find fossils. I look for treasure with old maps of fallen empires. I sit on the porch of my shack and write letters to my friends from the city, Bert and Juke and Minnie Bucket. Someday soon I will go and visit them.

In the afternoons, I listen to the wind from the empty spaces blow through the bristly pines.

I feel the soft loneliness of the world falling in shadow.

For the time being, I am happy here, here by myself at the Top of the World, all alone.

So I left.

Minnie was sweaty. "Come on!" she cried, tugging at my wrist.

"Here we come!" hollered Juke.

"Here we go!" giggled Bert, gnashing his teeth and rending his shirt.

"Um," I said. "Um, I think it's time for me to go." I lifted the sparkler-hat off my head. I turned off my shock-mittens. I rolled them up and gave them to Juke.

I said, "I've got to leave."

I said, "I miss the wind."

I hadn't slept for seven days. There now was a Ferris wheel over the gulf; there now was a towering tower; there now were some fireworks blasting the clouds, and statues that talked and that walked in the park.

Over the noise I cried to my friends. I yelled to them, "You know — I've been thinking. . . ."

"There's no time for thinking!" cried Shimmer from his podium, as the fairground lights in his beard flashed and whirled. "It's time for fun, for some funning, not thinking! Observe, folks, the End of the World! The splendid, resplendent, sublime view from here! Isn't it lovely! I'll build a new deck where you can eat dinner! I'll make you some go-carts! Some blimp-sleds! Some capsules! Whatever you wish, I will build! Gentlemen, ladies — drop what you're doing! There is not a moment for gloom or for thought! *We shall have FUN! That's FUN without END!*"

In the summer, the crowds were enormous and the inn was open for honeymoon couples who came for the smell of the emptiness and the four-hour sunsets, but the sunsets weren't clear through the haze on the boardwalk with all the lights from the games, which we played—Bert and me and Juke and Minnie Bucket.

We played Hurl the Gopher and Stumbling Ted; we played Bite the Bullet and Axe to the Grindstone and Blade-O-Matic Mumblypeg. We spun in the Gravitron till Bert got the dry heaves. We jumped from the ropes at the Shimmer Yow-Gulf-O-Drop. We hung in the ruins of the Sideways City, while sporty men in striped Shimmer Scramble-Sweaters bounded and vaulted from arches and domes.

"More fun! More fun!" bellowed Shimmer through his bullhorn, hung from a skyhook. "No solemn silences here at the End of the World! Nothing but laughter! And jumping! Madams, sirs—I highly recommend vertigo!"

Juke and Bert and Minnie Bucket came again in the spring.
We couldn't hear the wind whistling through the bristly pines.
The noise of the parties was too loud in the woods. Men with
mustaches gave fox-trot lessons to duchesses and dry-cleaning
heiresses wound up in silk. The monsters did not come up for the
lightning during spring rains anymore. They were afraid of the
noise and the engines. Bert and Juke and Minnie Bucket and I ran
on the paths through the woods, paths littered with noise-sticks
and razzers and horns. We played hide-and-go-seek and tip-the-
whole-hoosegow.

The shack where I lived was surrounded by buggies. I could
no longer find the bones of long monsters; I could no longer find
ancient gold. The pavilions and escalators covered them up.

In the winter, snow fell on the trees and the cliffs and the tombs. I watched the flakes fall silent on the land. One day, a sleigh pulled up, and there were Minnie Bucket and Bert and Juke. We spat in our hands and shook and we winked.

We had a great time. We watched shadow puppets at night while wind blew. We rented ice skates from the Shimmer O-Frost-A-Thon and made figure eights by the Rumblous Tumble-Up Falls and figure nines on the Lake at the Drop. People were screaming and swinging on pines. Guests now were skating and skiing in numbers, flashing down slopes to great jumps and long ramps.

"What is fun? *This* is fun!" cried Shimmer from shore. "Fun chock-a-block to your eyes and your teeth! Loneliness, ladies and lads? Gone, all gone at the Shimmer Inn Wintertime Ski and Skating Extravagorganza!"

And when the colors were really bright, Bert and Juke and Minnie Bucket came back from the city, and we ran through the Inn at the End of the World, and we played with the elevators, and they sent out for room-service turkey and chitlins and gum.

We rented four gliders from Shimmer's Hang-Glidery, and swooped from the cliffs at the end of the earth. We screamed as the blood all rushed to our feet.

"Stash your tears!" cried Shimmer from land. "Put aside mope! It is time now for fun! Ladies and gentlemen, hop into line! Swoop for today and forget your tomorrow!"

As the fall came, Constantine Shimmer finished his inn.
He put on the gables and porches and steeples. One by one, the
leaves fell from trees and drifted off the edge. I liked to watch
them spinning there. They fell through the sky under my feet.

So we spent the day in the woods by the cliffs. We spat and we clapped. I pointed to fossils. I showed them the paths. I showed them the trees. I showed them the footprints from slithery beasties.

When the time came for them to go back to the city, they said, "We don't want to leave. We'll come again. We'll see you soon. We'll be here this fall at the Inn at the End of the World."

But then I looked at the kids who stood around Shimmer. They were smiling and nice. They held out their hands. One was named Bert, and one was named Juke, and one was named Minnie Bucket. They wanted to like me. I wanted to like them. I started to smile.

"Well," I said. "Actually . . ."

Mr. Shimmer nodded.

I said to the kids, "What can I show you?"

"What do you do around here?" they asked.

I thought of what I did: fossils, sunsets. "Um," I said. Whistling. The gristle. The bristly pines. "Er . . ." I tried to think of something that might be exciting. "Well, if you spit off the edge of the earth, the spit gob goes forever," I said.

"Wow," said Bert, and "Zowie!" said Juke, and Minnie Bucket cried, "This is electric!"

A week later, I was netting fish that flew over the Rumblous Tumble-Up Falls when I heard big machines and men giving orders. They were paving a clearing. They were digging ditches. And tall Mr. Shimmer was leading a tour.

"Here," said Shimmer, "is the End of the World. Here is the cliff. Here is a lonely local boy with his mule. Notice their misty-eyed look. And here is the future site of the Inn at the End of the World."

I stood stock still. There was a little crowd, parents and children, staring at me and the End of the World. They gawked at the cliff.

I could not believe he had flattened the ground. "Mr. Shimmer?" I piped. "Mr. Constantine Shimmer?" I pointed to the paving stones. "What are you doing? What have you done?"

"I've brought you some friends," said Constantine Shimmer. "If you show them the sights, I will give you a shiny doubloon."

"Sights?" I said. "I just live here alone in a shack. I don't need friends and I don't need . . ."

Until one day. That day as I sat, dangling my legs off the world's edge to make my hair stand on end, I saw a strange man. He was a long-leggedy man with a wide, wide hat and a beard in a circle around his head. His glasses reflected the clouds.

He set up an easel. He drew out his brush from his boot. He painted the sky and the loneliest pine. And he said in a voice like wool from dream-sheep, "I am named Mr. Shimmer. Professional Visionary." He looked me up and looked me down. He said, "Boy, what do you do all day by the world's end?"

"Oh, sir," I said, "lots of things." And I told him about whistling, gristle, and watching the bristly pines.

"That's all?" asked Shimmer. He looked bored. "Don't you have fun? Don't you have friends?"

I looked at my feet. It had always seemed fun. But now, I didn't know.

"I think," said Shimmer, "things are going to change around here."

Over his picture of the cliff and the loneliest pine, he painted the words CONSTANTINE SHIMMER'S GALVANO-MAGICAL END OF THE WORLD TOURS. FUN ALL THE TIME!

On loud, stormy nights, I liked my shack. I liked to lie cozy near the brass-bellied stove, and hear the rain and the thunder fall, and the chuckling beasts with long tails or five legs or big kissing mouths squirm over the edge to go snapping at lightning. I was never afraid. I would fall asleep, hearing them growl in voices like plumbing. I knew that in the morning, there would be no sign of the rain but a mist, thick in the trees by the desolate cliffs. I was happy there all by myself, alone at the End of the World.

The days were slow and fine. I looked for treasure with old maps from fallen empires. I dusted off rocks and found fossils. I put the bones of long monsters back together with twine. I played ball by the drop. I sat and I read. I liked to listen to wind from the empty spaces blow through the bristly pines. The branches swayed in the blue. I ate hardtack and gristle. At sunset, I whistled dance tunes to the mule.

I lived by myself at the End of the World.

Me, All Alone, at the End of the World

M. T. Anderson

illustrated by

Kevin Hawkes

CANDLEWICK PRESS
CAMBRIDGE, MASSACHUSETTS

To my cousin Mark,
who took me hang-gliding
at the End of the World
M. T. A.

To Hugh and Joyce,
extraordinary cliff dwellers
K. H.

Text copyright © 2005 by M. T. Anderson
Illustrations copyright © 2005 by Kevin Hawkes

First edition 2005

Library of Congress Cataloging-in-Publication Data

Anderson, M. T.
Me, all alone, at the end of the world / M. T. Anderson ; illustrated by Kevin Hawkes. — 1st ed. 2005
p.   cm.
Summary: A boy enjoys living quietly by himself at the End of the World until
Mr. Constantine Shimmer, "Professional Visionary," builds an inn and an
amusement park, demanding that tourists come and have "Fun Without End!"
ISBN 0-7636-1586-2
[1. Solitude—Fiction. 2. Amusement parks—Fiction.] I. Hawkes, Kevin, ill. II. Title.
PZ7.A54395Ju 2005

[Fic]—dc21   2002034858

2 4 6 8 10 9 7 5 3 1

Printed in China

This book was typeset in Quercus.
The illustrations were done in watercolor and acrylic.

Candlewick Press
2067 Massachusetts Avenue
Cambridge, Massachusetts 02140

visit us at www.candlewick.com